TOWER HAMLETS PUBLIC LIBRARY

C001278180

KT-412-569

Library Learning Information

Idea Store® Bow
1 Gladstone Place
Roman Road
London E3 5ES

020 7364 4332

Created and managed by
Tower Hamlets Council

Acknowledgements

Cover design: Oliver Heath, Rafters Design

Illustration on page 20 © Paul Gardiner, 2005. The right of Paul Gardiner to be identified as the illustrator of this work has been asserted by him in accordance with the Copyright, Design and Patents Act, 1988.

Brinsford books are a direct result of the findings of a two-year authoring/research project with young offenders at HMYOI Brinsford, near Wolverhampton. Grateful thanks go to all the young people who participated so enthusiastically in the project and to Judy Jackson and Brian Eccleshall of Dudley College of Technology.

Copyright © Axis Education 2005

All rights reserved; no part of this publication my be reproduced, stored in a retrieval system, transmitted in any form, or by any means, electronic, mechanical, photocopying, recording, or otherwise, without the prior written permission of the publisher.

First published in Great Britain by Axis Education Ltd

ISBN 1-84618-007-4

Axis Education PO Box 459
Shrewsbury SY4 4WZ

Email: enquiries@axiseducation.co.uk

www.axiseducation.co.uk

Chapter One

Lenford picked up two packets of crisps, a bottle of pop and an apple from the counter. He shoved them into his school bag and walked out of the shop. As he shut the door behind him he saw a group of boys. There were always boys outside the shop. He did not think anything of it.

As he walked to school the boys were following him. He still did not think anything of it. They were heading for school, just like him.

But they did not talk like normal boys. They were silent. And they came nearer.

Lenford began to feel funny. He walked faster. So did the gang of boys. He started to run. So did they.

"Look what we've got here." One of them was right by his shoulder. "A right greedy little weed. Hand over your tuck."

The boys began to prod and poke Lenford, and then to punch him. He was too small to stop them. What else could he do? He handed over his tuck.

The boys ran in front now, laughing. One looked over his shoulder and shouted, "Make sure you've got plenty tomorrow. We'll be waiting for you!"

Lenford followed, miserable and scared.

Tower Hamlets	
Suppliers Code	AVA
Price	£4.95
Invoice Date	01/11/2006
LOC	BOW
Class	428.6
Barcode	C001278180

He was late for school. "Go straight to the Head's office and explain why," said the duty teacher. It was a really bad day.

He stood in front of the Head, staring down at the carpet beneath his feet. Mr Collins sounded disappointed. "It isn't like you to be late, Lenford. What happened?" Lenford went on staring at the carpet. He couldn't tell. If he did, they would get him again.

"Look at me when I talk to you, boy." Mr Collins began to sound angry. But as Lenford looked up his tone changed. "Why are you crying? What happened?"

He couldn't help it. He even told Mr Collins the boys' names. "I'll phone your parents now," said Mr Collins.

"They're not ... They're not at home," stammered Lenford. "Dad's at work and Mum works mornings."

"Then I'll write to them. They need to make a complaint so that I can take official action. Collect the letter at lunch time." Mr Collins smiled at Lenford. "Now get back to your classroom."

At least he was safe in his own classroom. He began to feel less upset. At lunchtime he went for his letter. But as he walked into the toilets after lunch he saw the same gang. He tried to leave quickly, but they grabbed him.

"You been squealing on us, you grass?" The biggest boy flicked ash from his cigarette into Lenford's face. "Let's give him a wash to show him what grassing means."

The gang grabbed Lenford and forced him to his knees. One of them pushed his head into the toilet bowl. He could smell the stench of old and new urine. Before he could throw up, the chain was pulled and water gushed over him. He breathed it in and started to choke. He was going to drown!

At last the noise of gushing water stopped. Lenford stopped coughing and spluttering. He sat on the dirty concrete floor. He'd had enough!

He picked up his bag and headed for home.

When Lenford reached his front gate he took a deep breath. He could still taste the foul water from the toilet. What would his parents do? They thought he was too soft at the best of times because he was always reading books.

He took another deep breath and took the front door key out of his bag. Once inside he put the letter on the kitchen table and shot upstairs to change his clothes. His mum would go mad if she saw the state his clothes were in.

She was back early today. There was a silence from the kitchen. And then her feet pounded the stairs.

"What the heck is all this about? I'm not going to no school. You know we never go up the school. Can't stand those stuck-up teachers. You've just got to stand up for yourself. Stop letting those kids bully you. Sort yourself out. It's your own fault. You're such a wimp!"

When his dad got home, Lenford got more of the same, plus a smack round the head.

He knew he couldn't stop the gang. Not after that stuff in the toilet. All he could think was, "One day, I'll be big and strong. I'll get my own back on everyone then."

Chapter Two

Lenford, PJ, Raz and Shoes parked their bikes in front of the shops. PJ fetched them all pie and chips. Raz got the fags. Lenford and Shoes waited by the bikes. As they finished their lunch, a group of younger boys appeared from round the corner.

"Look what we've got here, boys. Our own personal cash machines." Lenford and Shoes walked across to the boys with their hands out. The boys silently handed over their cash. They looked dejected and turned to leave.

"Hang on." Raz grabbed the bag of one of them and opened it up. "Thought so. I saw him playing with his PlayStation 2 this morning. I guess it's our turn now." Raz laughed as he took it out.

"That was my birthday present. My mum will go mad if I don't take it home."

"Happy Birthday," said Lenford. "Have a nice day. We will."

The others sniggered.

"I'll tell ..."

Lenford's eyes bored into the younger boy. "You know better than to tell anyone. Now clear off."

The boys fled.

Lenford looked thoughtful. "We'll need to stash this until later. Then we can sell it. It's got to be worth fifty quid. We can buy some buda. PJ – your place is the closest. Dump it at yours until later. Meet you back at school."

Mrs Parker, Headmistress of their secondary school, was waiting for the four of them as they wheeled their bikes into the shed.

"My office," she said sharply. "Now! I want to talk to you lot." As she opened the door of her office they saw two uniformed police. PJ and Shoes turned around and ran for it, but Lenford and Raz couldn't get out.

"Right. What's been going on at lunchtime? I'm told you took Perkins' PlayStation from him by force. His mother has been on the phone."

I'll get him for that, Lenford swore to himself. But on the outside he looked wide-eyed innocent. "Us? It's a load of rubbish. We ain't done nothing." The kid must have gone straight home to tell his mother. The cops hadn't half got here quick!

"Why should Perkins tell his mother if it didn't happen? He has no reason to make it up. Listen, Lenford – and you, James – we've had your little lot marked out as bullies from the first day you arrived. Now we have some real evidence."

"Look, I tell you, we ain't done nothing! That kid's lost it and made up a story. We never took his PlayStation, nor his money neither." One of the policemen moved forward. "Money? I don't remember Mrs Parker saying anything about money. I think you two had better come down to the police station with us. We need to take a statement from you."

"But ..." began Raz.

"Don't worry." Mrs Parker's eyes were hard. "Your friends will get the same treatment when they turn up. We will not tolerate this kind of behaviour at our school."

After giving their statements and receiving a caution each, Lenford and Raz met Wilson, their dope supplier, at the Community Centre to score some buda. Then they headed off to the park to smoke it. PJ and Shoes came shiftily out of the bushes.

"You two had your cautions?" Lenford looked at them. "If not, you'd better go and get it done tomorrow. You don't want to be picked up at the wrong time."

"Yeah." PJ smiled. "I've lost count how many I've had. My Mum will go ape – as usual."

"My Dad just whacked me for getting caught." Lenford rubbed his cheek, remembering the blow.

"This'll take care of your pain, Len." Raz smiled as they shared out the weed and started to roll spliffs. "Good job they didn't find the evidence."

"You know we could buy in bulk off Wilson and flog the stuff round school. We could get a mobile too and pass the number round." Lenford liked his idea. "We'd have as much as we want to smoke ourselves then."

"Great idea. Let's do it." Then Shoes' enthusiasm turned to doubt. "What if we get caught?"

"Nah, Shoes. We won't get caught. We're too clever for that."

Chapter Three

"Shit! It's the cops! Get a move on. They're on to us."

"Maybe we should have walked home from the club, or took a taxi." PJ laughed nervously.

"No time for regrets. Turn down that street. Try to lose them. Quick. Cut into the estate across the playing field. They won't follow us there. Shit. They have. For God's sake, put your foot down. They're gaining. Oh, no!"

Lenford swallowed hard as he saw the second police car waiting for them.

"Sorry, Len. Not much of a chase, was it?" PJ looked worried.

"Nah, PJ. No worries." Lenford smiled reassuringly at PJ as the coppers came towards them. "May have to do some gardening for old ladies or something. This is a bit past a caution."

"Aha, it's you two. Just as we thought." The big man in blue smiled with satisfaction. "We've been after you lot for a long time. Pity we didn't get the whole bunch."

"Why would you want us, officer?" Lenford smiled cheekily at the policeman.

"Just because we 'borrowed' a ride home? It's hardly worth your time doing the paperwork. It's not even scratched."

"Oh, we'll have you for the car as well." The officer grinned again. "But most of all it'll be good to stop you selling dope to little kids."

Lenford's face fell. He'd forgotten the cannabis! How could he? He'd got an ounce in his pocket and another three in the glove compartment. He'd be hard put to explain that away as personal use. He'd have to phone Shoes and tell him to move the rest of the stuff out of his yard. And to send him a solicitor at the same time.

The interview room was stuffy.

"I ain't saying a word till my brief gets here. And my parents. I'm only sixteen, so you have to tell them too."

Lenford dreaded his mum and dad arriving, but needed to buy some time. "I want my free phone call too."

"Okay, son. Interview suspended at 02.10 hours." The sergeant switched off the machine and took Lenford to the phone booth in the corridor. "Yeah, I know the call is private. You've got three minutes. Okay?"

He walked to the Gents to leave Lenford to make his call. Lenford dialled the number. "Shoes? Yeah, it's me. Look, listen. Me and PJ have been arrested. Go round to mine and flush the stuff down the loo. If they find that I'm stuffed. Nah, just tell my Mum and Dad you've got to get something for me. Oh, and get me a brief – a good one. They've found four ounces already."

He slammed the phone down just as the sergeant came out of the Gents, laughing happily.

"You're too late, son. We've already sent a team with a search warrant. Your dad's on his way here. Your mum's staying at home to make sure we don't damage anything. You're going down, son. At least four years if there's much more at home."

Too late, Lenford saw the open windows at the top of the corridor wall. He'd been too busy talking to Shoes to notice.

The solicitor was a good one. He got two years.

Chapter Four

"You took those biscuits off Jones, I know you did. It's a good job you're out on Friday. If you were staying I'd have you down the block for a few weeks. You might let other people's property alone then. Your sort makes me sick."

Lenford leant insolently against the wall and smiled at the screw. He looked the man straight in the eyes, then took a cookie from his packet and bit a chunk out of it.

"Yum, this tastes good."

"Get behind your door. You're just a cheap bully."

On Friday Lenford strutted through the big gate. Shoes and PJ shouted him over to the car.

"Want a blow? Here's a splitz." Shoes handed him a big spliff as the three of them piled into the Subaru.

Lenford ran his hand over the Colin McRae interior admiringly. "New wheels. Hot or legal?"

PJ laughed. "It's legal, man – bought and paid for. Since you've been away Shoes is selling big time. We're making enough money now. Big time."

"It's heavy to be back on the road," said Lenford. He leaned back into the springy seat. The air smelled sweet.

"What do you think of the house? It's running smoothly, ain't it? The girls are good – loadsa custom. I've got a great opportunity for you."

"What do you mean, opportunity? You think I should help you run the girls?"

"I need to leave town for a while. If we can cut a deal, you can have the girls and I can have some extra cash."

The air smelled even sweeter. And there would be other opportunities. They needed to pay a visit to JB, first thing.

Chapter Five

"We're making loads of jed," said Lenford. "Got the buda and the girls. It's sweet, man."

JB looked at him shrewdly. "You interested in a bit more? I could put you in touch with the main man – but not for the scully. Big D deals with top shit."

Lenford looked at Shoes, PJ and Wilson. "What do you think we should do?"

"Let's go for it." Shoes looked at Lenford. "We'll need gats for when it goes down."

JB smiled. "I can put you in touch with someone who can help you there, too."

An hour later they had found Raz. He was their best driver. He pulled up at the warehouse.

"This is spooky, man. It's much too soon."

Lenford smiled at him. "You've got to come with us. We're gonna need six."

"No way. I'm the driver. That's what I do. I can't do this stuff."

Lenford handed a 9mm over. "Take this. It'll help you do the business."

Raz held it in his hand. He shrugged, swallowed, then muttered, "Okay, man." His hands shook as he stuck the gun in the waistband at the back of his trousers.

The six lads strolled into the dark, echoing warehouse. At first, all they could see was a black lump at the far end. As they drew nearer the lump began to turn into Big D.

Raz's voice shook as he whispered, "This is way too deep. You see who we're doing business with here? That's Nails and CK. They work for Big D. Man, it's too much."

Lenford shushed him. Raz shook a bit more.

Lenford and Wilson slouched up to Nails, hands in pockets, trying to look cool. Trying to calm their nerves.

"What you got for us, man?" said Lenford.

Nails opened the palm of his hand. A small bag lay in its centre. "We can let you have an ounce for starters, plus some crack. Seventeen fifty?"

Wilson put out his hand. "I taste it first – I'm a kind of expert." He placed the tip of his finger in the bag and rubbed the powder onto his front teeth. He started to spit. "That's shit! You're trying to rip us off. I know brown and that don't taste like no brown I ever took."

CK grabbed his arm. "You stupid shit. It's good stuff. It's purer than what you get on the street."

Raz whipped the gun out of his trousers. "You think you can treat us like shit because we're young. You're wrong. This tells you you're wrong!" His hand shook and his forehead was covered in sweat.

Nails drew his gun and pointed it at Raz. "Put it down, you stupid kid."

"Who are you calling a stupid kid? I ..."

The noise echoed on and on, round the empty warehouse. Big D grabbed Nails. Nails gasped. "I'm sorry, boss. I thought he was gonna ..."

"Never mind thinking. You're obviously no good at that. Get us out of here. The kid's dead."

Raz was a small, crumpled heap in a dark pool. There was no spark left in him. Lenford assumed the rest of the gang were following him as he legged it.

Shoes jumped into the driving seat. He was the only one who had realised they had no driver.

Chapter Six

Lenford was still shaking when he got home. His face was grey and he avoided his mum's gaze when he entered the kitchen.

"What's up with you, you miserable sod?"

He thought about lying. No good. He just had to tell someone. His mum sat down.

"You're in deep, Lenford. Something seriously dodgy. I can't believe it. Whatever it is, son, stop it. Now. You could end up like Raz."

Lenford shrugged and left the room. Why start caring now, Mum? He had to tell Raz's Mum. But it shouldn't really be done on the phone. There was nothing else for it – he'd have to go and see her.

The two minute walk to Raz's house took forever. It was all his fault. They'd been too greedy. Raz hadn't wanted to get that involved. And now he had to tell his mum that he was dead.

As Lenford turned the corner he saw familiar flashing blue lights and realised he was too late. The police had got there first. He caught a glimpse of Raz's mum's tear-stained face through the window as the cop car sped off.

Two weeks later the date of Raz's funeral arrived. Lenford pulled up at the red brick church. There was already quite a crowd. All dressed in black. Lenford had on his black Moschino suit. He knew he looked sharp, but inside he felt like shit. He'd been the same since Raz died. What a mess.

Lenford forced back the tears when Raz turned up in an all-white coffin covered in lilies. Lenford, PJ, and Shoes were pall-bearers. Raz felt light above their shoulders. The service was a blur. Lenford blanked out the hymns, the tissues and the tears of raw grief.

Afterwards they all filed back to their cars. He noticed Raz's cousin didn't have a ride.

"Hey, Lucy – want a lift?" Lenford had always had an eye for Lucy from afar. She was a fine-looking woman.

"Thanks, Len."

They made small talk about the funeral. Then Lucy changed the subject. "That's a nice motor for someone your age."

"Got a good job. Pays good money."

"What do you do?"

"This and that really, nothing too exciting." Not much! He could hardly tell Lucy what he really did. They carried on chatting for the rest of the twenty-minute journey. By the time they got to Lucy's house, Lenford felt he'd known the girl all his life. He was sure she felt the same way.

The house was full of relatives and friends. They were eating and drinking, but it was all very subdued. Lenford stayed and stayed. He wanted to catch Lucy again on her own. Finally she was free. They talked about everything – his family, her family, Raz and how much they both missed him. They seemed to discuss everything apart from Lenford's real line of work. That could wait.

They had been so engrossed in each other that they didn't realise everyone else had left. It was late. Lucy asked him to stay. He kissed her gently. "Are you sure?"

"Yes, really I am. I like you, Lenford. I like you a lot."

Lenford turned out the hall light as Lucy led him upstairs.

He woke early. Lucy was curled up next to him. Her naked body was warm and she looked beautiful. Lenford couldn't stop smiling. He held her in his arms and kissed her lightly on the forehead. He searched for a scrap of paper in his jeans pocket and scribbled his mobile number on it. Then he crept out of bed quietly and left the paper by her side.

Fantastic. She was just fantastic. This was the start of something really good. He just knew it.

At home he showered and changed. He bumped into his mum on the stairs.

"Where have you been?"

"Nowhere. I was busy."

"Lenford ..."

He slammed the door shut so that he didn't have to listen to the rest. He leapt into his car and headed for Wilson's house. There were deals to be done.

Wilson was waiting for him. "My phone's been hot, man. Yours too?" Lenford reached into his pocket for the phone. "Idiot – it's not switched on," he cursed himself. Then he slapped each pocket in panic. The gun. It must be on his bed. "Wilson, I've gotta go home. The gun's there. I'll only be ten minutes."

He sped off, leaving Wilson clutching Lenford's new Nokia.

Seconds after Lenford left the Nokia rang.

"Hi, where are you?" asked a high-pitched voice.

"At the house," said Wilson. "What do you want?"

"I don't know. I ..."

Wilson interrupted her. No time for time-wasters. "Ten, twenty, thirty. I've got it all."

"What do you mean, you've got it all?"

"Crack, smack, the lot. You want it – we've got it."

Lucy hung up. Drugs. That was where his money came from. The bastard!

Chapter Seven

Business was good and Lenford had been busy. It had been six days since he saw Lucy but he hadn't stopped thinking about her. He dialled her number.

"How are you, sweets? You been avoiding me?"

"I wondered when you'd crawl out from under your stone."

"What?" Lenford was confused.

"When I called, your mate was using your phone to push drugs. Is that what you do, Len? Is that where all the money comes from?" Her voice got higher and higher.

"Lucy, listen ..."

"No. You listen. I'm not interested in seeing a drug dealer. I know you were involved in Raz's death."

"It wasn't like that, Lucy. I really like you. I think I love you. Please ..."

She cut him off in mid-sentence. "It's easy, Lenford. If you do like me, you'll give up drugs and crime."

The line went dead.

Lenford was in turmoil. But he knew what he had to do. He couldn't live without Lucy. He was going to prove himself to her. He had plenty of money and he could put it to good use. He could run a good business – he just had to find one that was legal.

What could he do? Nothing boring. Something fun. Something fun that would earn him money.

What was he good at? Nothing. He had no qualifications. The only thing he could do really well was play on a PlayStation. Some skill!

And then it struck him. Of course. An amusement arcade. He would set up an arcade where kids would come and spend money.

Three weeks later the deal was done. He'd found premises, rented the machines and was looking for staff. He'd show Lucy he meant business.

Nervously, Lenford called her. "Hi Lucy."

"Look, I told you ..."

"No, listen. I'm calling to offer you a job. A real job. In my amusement arcade. I'm opening on Friday. Why don't you come round and see for yourself?"

Lucy didn't think she was going to go. But curiosity got the better of her. She walked into the arcade and found Lenford sitting at a desk in the office.

Lenford beamed when he saw her. "You won't regret coming, Lucy." But his face fell as he looked over her shoulder. Shoes sauntered in, hands in pockets.

"Legal, then? I knew it." She turned to leave.

His heart sank.

"Where you been, boy?"

"Busy, setting up here. I told you, man. I'm not into it no more."

"Come on, Lenford. You'll never give it up."

"Look, I mean it. This is me now. My future's here at the arcade. I like it. It's safe and it'll make good money."

"Why are you going fool, fool?"

"What do you mean fool, fool? You expect me to carry on with drugs when I got a beautiful girl like this?"

Shoes sucked his teeth and walked off in disgust. Lucy looked at Lenford.

"You've been doing all this for me? Is that how much you really love me?"

"Obvious. You're the best thing in my life."

He looked at her shyly and grabbed her round the waist.

Two months later the amusement arcade was building trade. Lenford had been working there night and day. Lucy had hardly seen him. And she had some news. She was scared but excited. And it had to be told. She was pregnant. It had happened the night of Raz's funeral. She looked up at Lenford after she told him.

"I can't believe it," said Lenford.

Lucy's face fell.

"No, no. Don't get me wrong. Are you sure? Of course you're sure. We're having a baby. Are we? I mean, do you want to keep it?"

"Do you?"

"Yeah. I want to be with you and the baby for the rest of my life. Do you want to be my wife?"

Lucy flung her arms round his neck and burst into tears. "Yes, yes."

The wedding came only a month later. Everything was going fine. Lenford's heart nearly burst when he saw Lucy walk down the aisle in the church. She looked beautiful. He was a lucky man. He had Lucy and a baby on the way.

What a day!

It didn't bother him that his parents refused to come. So what was new? But Lucy's turned up, and a few friends. They had wanted it to be a small affair. They'd make up for it with a big honeymoon. The arcade was doing really well and he'd found someone he trusted to be manager for a while.

Lucy thought they were going to Majorca for a week. But when they arrived at the airport he handed Lucy the tickets with a daft grin.

"What have you done?" she gasped. "Hawaii? You're mad! Oh, Lenford, that's fantastic. You know I've always wanted to go there. It's going to be perfect."

Chapter Eight

The honeymoon was perfect, but there were unwelcome rumblings on Lenford's return. Not with the arcade. The new manager seemed to have done his stuff well, but Lenford wanted to be quite sure. He was still checking on the paperwork after closing time when the phone rang.

"Hello. Raz's Amusements."

"Coming over?" said Shoes.

"Nah, man. Can't. I'm spending time here and with the Missis."

"What do you mean, time with the Missis? You just spent two weeks on honeymoon with her!"

Shoes hung up.

PJ rang next.

"Don't ever see you now, cuz."

"Yeah, P. Had a heavy honeymoon."

"Yeah? The lads need to see you, man. Something's going on big time."

"What do you mean?"

"The house is going up. And there seem to be a whole lotta guys after us."

"I can give you some cash to get out of the country."

"I don't want no cash. What about the rest of the gang?"

"You're my cousin and I'm looking out for you. The gang don't mean nothing to me."

PJ hung up.

Lenford was getting fed up with this. He was just about to switch the phone off when Shoes rang. Shoes had taken over the gang when Lenford left.

"What the fuck do you mean? The gang don't mean nothing to you?"

"Look, I'm out of it. I've got Lucy. The business. And a kid on the way. I ain't got time for it, man."

Lenford hung up before Shoes could get there first. He turned his phone off and slammed it on the table. Damn them. Couldn't they see he just didn't want to see them any more? If Lucy heard him talking to them she'd go mad. He'd go home and turn off the phone there as well.

The car park was deserted apart from a smart black Mercedes M350 four by four. It was Shoes waiting for him. He looked worried. And angry.

Lenford was just fed up with them all.

"There's people after us, man," said Shoes. "We need your help."

"I'm out of that now. I told you."

"Look, we need some straps and some gats. We need some protection."

"Nah. I just can't do it."

"What do you mean, you can't do it? You're one of us, man."

"Nah. I was one of you."

Shoes had always had a temper. He lunged at Lenford and clipped him on the chin with a clenched fist. Lenford staggered backwards and tripped over a chair. He landed on the floor with a thud. Shoes said nothing as he left.

Lenford saw him pull away in his Merc.

The next afternoon Lenford opened the doors to his public at 4 pm. Friday nights were always busy. He went back to the office to tidy up last night's paperwork. Bright white headlamps caught his attention. He looked out of the window. The blacked-out windows of the M350 wound down as the car screeched to a halt right outside his window. Lenford squinted. The unmistakeable barrel of a shotgun was pointing right at him.

The windows smashed as the first bullets hit it. Lenford didn't see the bullet that got him square in the chest. Shards of glass showered the office. His body slumped to the floor. He was dead before he hit it. The car sped off. The only sound was the warm blood gurgling in Lenford's throat.

Epilogue

Five months after Lenford died Lucy gave birth to a baby boy. She named him after his father. Lucy runs the arcade now, but never sees the gang.

No one was ever prosecuted for Lenford's murder.

Glossary

brief	solicitor
brown	heroin
buda	cannabis
dope	cannabis
gats	guns
jed	money
screw	prison officer
scully	cannabis
smack	heroin
splitz	spliff, cannabis cigarette